Bath New York Singapore Hong Kong Cologne Delhi Melbourne

This is the story of Bambi. You can
read along with me in your book.
You will know it is time to turn the
page when you hear the chimes ring
like this ...

Let's begin now:

It was spring, and the forest was alive with news. Everyone was excited.

"It's happened!"

"Have you heard?"

"Over in the thicket!"

"Come and see!"

A magpie flew by old Owl, who was taking his daily nap. "Wake up, friend Owl! The young prince is born! Come on! You'd better hurry!"

Now, Owl preferred to spend the day at home – fast asleep. But when he heard the news, he woke right up and flew to the thicket.

"After all, it isn't every day a young prince is born."

As the animals quietly approached the shady glen, they saw a newborn baby deer sleeping by his proud mother. She gently nudged the tiny fawn and whispered, "Wake up. You have visitors."

The fawn slowly opened his new eyes. Then he got up, his new legs still shaky, and looked around curiously at the creatures who had come to admire him.

A friendly baby rabbit named Thumper hopped over to the mother deer. "What're you going to call him?"

"I think I'll name him Bambi."

"Bambi? Yep, I guess that'll do."

Then Thumper and the other visitors hopped and scampered away, leaving the young prince to nap.

By the time summer came, Prince Bambi was strong enough to explore the forest with his mother. "Come along, Bambi," she said one morning. "It's time you learned your way outside the thicket." The little fawn, his legs steadier now, followed his mother out of the glen.

"Hello, young prince!" The chorus of voices came from above. Bambi looked up to see a possum family, hanging by their tails, as possums do. He was puzzled. Who were these upside-down folk? Bambi turned his head this way and that, trying to get a proper look at them.

Another voice came from nearby. "Hi, Bambi!" It was Thumper, who was eating clover with his family. "Let's go have some fun," suggested the little rabbit. That seemed like a fine idea, so Bambi trotted off after Thumper.

The two friends came upon some birds perched on a low branch. Bambi stared at them closely. "Those are birds," explained Thumper. "Say 'bird.'"

Bambi took a deep breath. "Bird!"

Thumper hopped up and down excitedly. "He talked! He talked! The young prince can talk!"

Then a butterfly landed on Bambi's tail. "Bird!" he said, feeling very proud of himself.

Thumper giggled. "That's not a bird. That's a butterfly!"

Bambi shook his head in confusion. Then he saw some more small, colourful things. Bending down, he sniffed at one. "Butterfly!"

Thumper smiled. "No, Bambi. That's a flower. It's pretty."

Just then, out from the flowers popped a black and white face with two bright eyes. "Pretty flower!" said Bambi.

No one had ever called a skunk that before. Thumper rocked with laughter. The bashful little skunk just smiled. "Oh, that's all right. He can call me Flower if he wants to. I don't mind."

Late that summer, Bambi's mother took him to the meadow. She moved carefully and sniffed the wind. "You must be very careful on the meadow, Bambi. Out there we are unprotected. There are no trees to hide us."

When his mother was sure it was safe, she let Bambi bound out onto the grassy meadow. He was surprised to see a little girl fawn about his own age. Her name was Faline, and she and Bambi soon became great friends.

One day in early fall, as Bambi and his friends were playing on the meadow, a mighty deer rushed out from the trees. It was the Forest King, and he signalled everyone to leave the meadow. In the distance, Bambi could hear the loud, frightening noise of guns.

Immediately, Bambi and his mother raced for the safety of the thicket. Bambi was frightened. When it became quiet again, he lifted his head. "I don't understand, Mother. Why did we run?"

Bambi's mother was still alertly watching the path from the meadow. Then she turned to her son. "Man… was in the forest."

One cold morning, Bambi awoke to a startling sight.
"Mother! What's all this white stuff?"
"Why, it's snow. Winter has come to the forest."
Bambi stepped out of the thicket carefully and was
surprised when his feet sank deep into the soft, white snow.

The fawn was delighted. The snow became a game. He pranced all about in the chilly air, leaving hoofprints in the snow.

From a nearby pond, Thumper called to him. "Hiya, Bambi! Come on over here. It's all right. See? The water's stiff!"

Bambi trotted confidently out onto the frozen pond. But as soon as his tiny hooves touched the ice, his hind legs slipped, and down he crashed.

Thumper laughed and laughed. "You have to watch both ends at the same time!" Bambi blinked his large eyes, got up carefully, and slid across the ice to Thumper. "Some fun, huh, Bambi?" They had a wonderful time.

The winter months passed slowly. Food became scarce, and Bambi's mother had to strip bark from the trees to eat.

"Winter is sure long, isn't it, Mother?"

"It seems long. But spring will be here soon."

At last the snow melted and spring came. Owl awoke from his nap. "My! If it isn't the young prince. How fine you look! And you've grown a pair of antlers."

Owl wasn't the only one who admired Bambi's new antlers. His childhood friend, Faline, also thought they were fine. She had grown up, too, and was now a graceful and lovely doe. She walked up to Bambi and touched noses.

Owl had warned the young deer about this very thing. Bambi fell in love with Faline. "They're twitterpated!" muttered Owl as he watched Faline and Bambi walking in the moonlight.

Months passed. Again came a time when Man entered the forest, bringing with him guns and fire.

Bambi sensed that something was wrong. He left Faline and went to the edge of a tall cliff. Looking down, he saw a campfire, and as he watched, a spark from that fire started some brush burning. The fire spread quickly.

Bambi hurried to warn Faline and the other animals. They all raced out of the forest. Down from the trees ran the squirrels, from under the ground scurried the ground hogs, away from their nests flew the birds.

Bambi and Faline joined the other creatures on a bank
across the wide river. They all watched sadly as the flames
destroyed their forest homes. But spring came again to the
forest, and green grass and flowers covered the scars left by
the fire.

Once again the air was alive with excitement. This time it
was friend Owl who spread the great news.

"Come quickly, everybody. To the thicket!" And all the
forest creatures rushed to see what had happened.

There was Faline, resting quietly with not one, but two new fawns.

Owl's great yellow eyes widened in surprise. "Look! Twins! And a healthier pair I've never seen. Prince Bambi must be mighty proud!"

Rabbits and squirrels, raccoons and birds looked on in awe.

One of the baby fawns stood up on his wobbly little legs. He tottered over to a clear space in the screen of trees and peered through the brush toward the edge of a great cliff. There stood Bambi, his father, now King of the Forest. Someday, this young prince would grow up and become king, just like his father.